For Nikulás

Albert copyright © Frances Lincoln Limited 2004
Text and illustrations copyright © Lani Yamamoto 2004

First published in Great Britain in 2004 by
Frances Lincoln Children's Books
4 Torriano Mews
Torriano Avenue
London NW5 2RZ

www.franceslincoln.com

British Library Cataloguing in Publication Data available on request

ISBN 1-84507-056-9

Printed in Singapore

9 8 7 6 5 4 3 2 1

It was raining again....

and Albert had already saved all the animals from the flood,

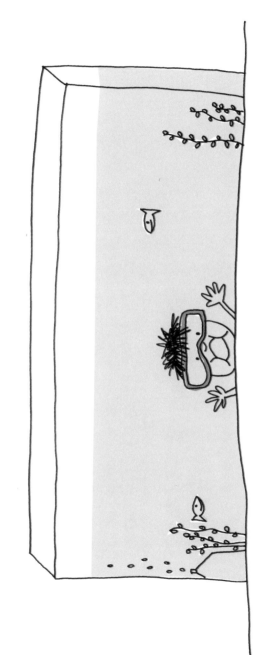

been swimming with the sharks,

and discovered the pirates' long lost treasure.

In fact, he had done everything. There was nothing left to do.

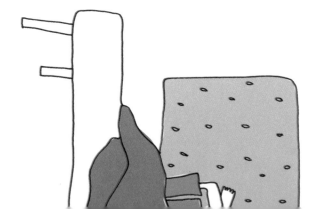

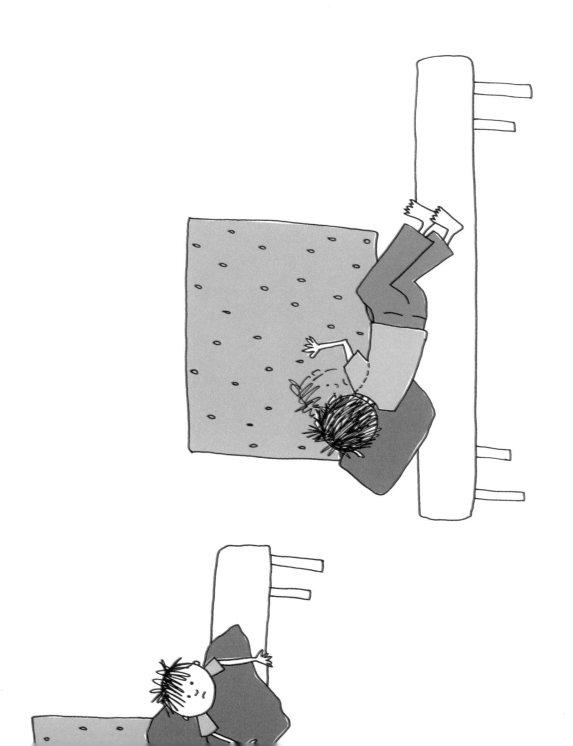

Outside, the raindrops were getting heavier and falling louder.

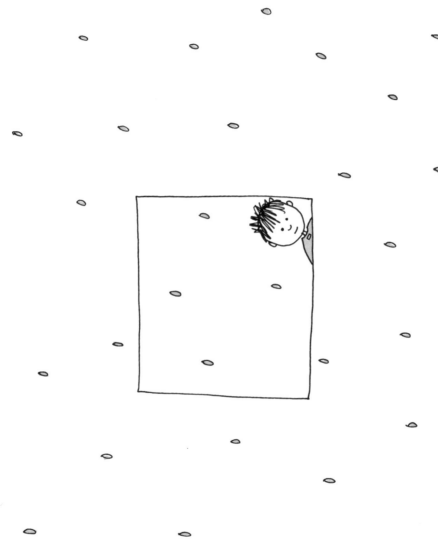

Albert began to think....

If I am in my house...

and my house is in the street....

near the park....

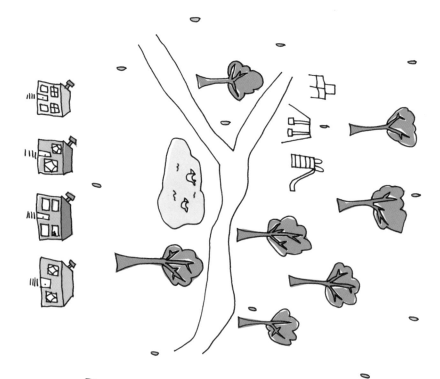

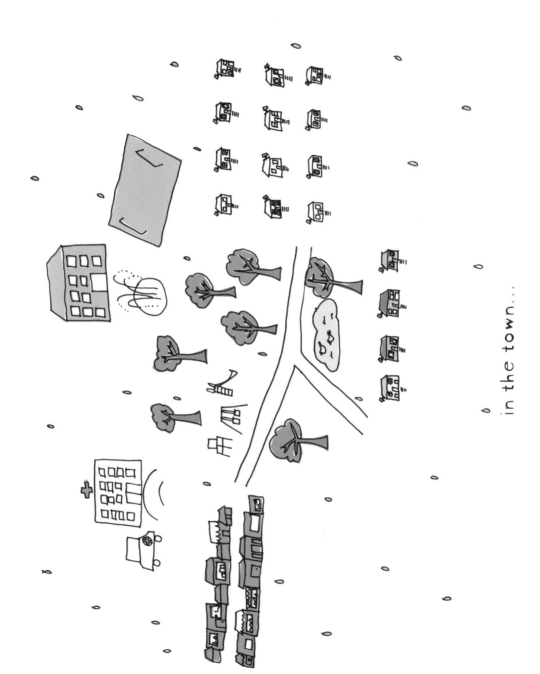

in the town....

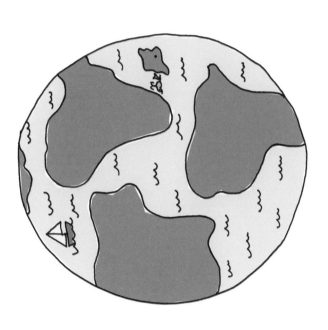

and the country is on the Earth....

and the Earth is among the stars and the planets...

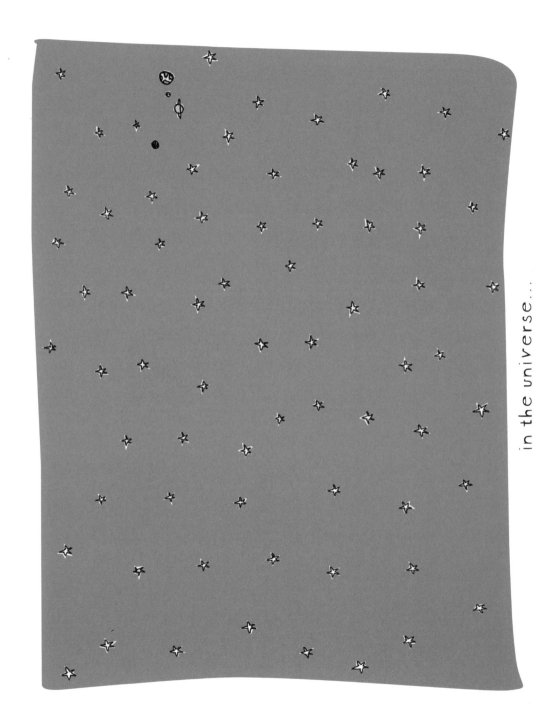

in the universe....

then what is the universe in?

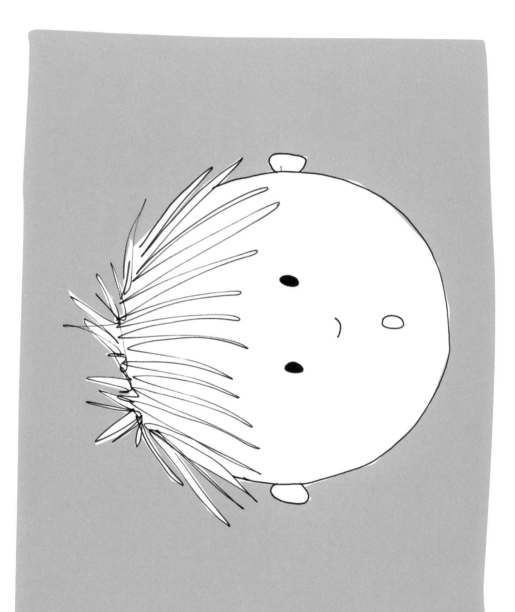

"What are you doing, darling?"
called Albert's mother from downstairs.

"Nothing, Mum!" said Albert with a smile.

But Albert was already on the way to his biggest adventure yet.